LISA RYAN CAMPBELL

ExO ExO

AN *ex* FILES CHRISTMAS

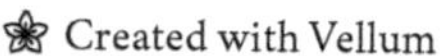 Created with Vellum

CHAPTER ONE

*W*ednesday, December 22nd

Roman sat in his car with the heat blasting to ward off the chill from outside. Soon, another car pulled up beside him and shut off its headlights. He looked over at the time on his dashboard and saw it was nearly 11:30 in the evening, which was about right. Dirty deals were never made during daylight hours. This was his first, and he wished he could say for certain it would be his last. But, like his ex-partner used to say, the first one was the hardest, but the rest got easier. Then one day you look up and you're swirling in corruption with no way out.

This deal involved FBI witness Dana McIntyre, Senator Pierce McIntyre's ex-wife. She was going to testify on his illegal dealings and hand over some bribery list in exchange for witness protection. Roman hadn't been involved in the case, but apparently, her original escort was held up in another state, and he was ordered to take on the job. To anyone else, having to escort a witness across state lines so close to Christmas would be an inconvenience, but he had nowhere to be until Christmas Day and Mrs. McIntyre would be at the safe house well before then. Also, the job came with overtime pay, which is something he desperately needed at the moment as he saved for a family lawyer retainer. Still, the little bit of money from his salary wouldn't be nearly enough to cover the cost of taking Kyra to court and demanding shared custody of his two children.

That's why he was sitting in this deserted parking garage with one other car. As soon as he accepted the job to escort Mrs. McIntyre to her new safe house, it was as if an invisible alarm had been tripped. Within an hour of him receiving his orders, he'd gotten a call with an offer he should have instantly refused, but didn't.

His passenger door opened and a man, appearing to be in his late 40's wearing a dark suit and coat climbed in, ushering in the cold air and the scent of his cologne with him. Before Roman could blink, the man brandished a small manila envelope that was no doubt padded with money. This would be the first time he put a face to the stranger who contacted him with this deal. Before this, they only communicated once through Roman's private email and then through text message. He never told Roman his name, but simply introduced himself as the Senator McIntyre's unofficial chief of staff, whatever the hell that meant.

"This is the first half," he said, handing it to Roman. "The rest will be waiting at the house."

Roman looked at the envelope in his hand and then turned to stare out the front window at the empty car spaces surrounding them. Once again, he was asking himself what the hell he was doing.

"She won't be harmed," the man said, obviously sensing his hesitation. "I can assure you that's not what this is about."

"Then explain it to me," Roman demanded as he turned to look at him. "If you're not going to hurt her or kill her, why do you want her? What am I setting her up for?"

The man sighed with impatience. 'We've been through this. My job is to protect the Senator's interests, and it's not in his best interest if she testifies or hands over that pay off list to the DA. All we need you to do is drive to the location in that envelope, pick up the rest of your money and drive on. Two men from the Senator's security detail will be waiting at the house, but you won't see them. They'll tail you and Mrs. McIntyre the rest of the way to the Seattle safe-house where you will hand her over to your fed buddies and leave."

That didn't appease Roman in the least. Finally, the man relented.

"All right, look. Between you and me, the Senator and his ex-wife divorced over his cheating. She caught him sticking his dick in some coed one too many times. Now that their marriage is over, she's still out for blood. Her testimony and that list she stole from him will humiliate and ruin him, and she knows that. She's taken this too far. He just wants to know where she is, so he can talk to her. He'll probably whisk her away to Bermuda or Tahiti. They'll make up, she'll go back to doing his finances again, and all of this will blow over." He paused and then added, "And you'll receive a hefty payday as a thank you."

"How will you get her away from FBI custody?"

"You let us worry about that. You'll be long gone and in the clear. You won't be suspected for a thing."

Roman thought about it. Maybe all of this really was the actions of an angry ex-wife. As long as she wouldn't be hurt in any way, he could do as they ask, take their money and hire the best lawyer he could find that would get him equal time with Tyler and Brianna.

Thinking of his children, he held the money tight in his hands and prayed nothing would go wrong. He prayed even harder that he was being a good dad.

* * *

The man named Alex sat in his car watching as Agent Roman Walsh drove away with the money. His SUV exited the parking garage and when Alex could no longer see his taillights, he reached into his pocket, pulled out his cell and dialed a number.

"Hey, it's me. Walsh went for it."

He paused, listening to the response on the other end.

"What do you mean you're surprised? I'm not. His partner was dirty. Why shouldn't he be dirty, too?"

The other caller spoke and Alex nodded.

"Yeah, he took the money. Get ready, because you're on." He chuckled. "If all goes well, you'll be getting your Christmas present early this year."

CHAPTER TWO

hursday, December 23rd

Roman pulled up to the two-story townhome in Pacific Heights and got out of his car. He walked up the stone steps to the glass and wrought iron door and rang the bell. An elegant chime rang from inside, and he took a moment to turn and look down the quiet tree-lined street. It was still early morning and people were out getting in their morning run, with and without the dog. New moms walked the streets, bundled up in thick coats pushing carriages with newborns and toddlers. Some even had those contraptions that attached the baby to the front of their chest and Roman felt a familiar ache when he saw that. When Kyra was pregnant with Tyler, they'd take walks together, and he'd have Brianna strapped to his chest—her tiny infant body softly bouncing as they did their morning stroll. His children were now seven and six, and he woke every morning wondering what memories he was missing out on now that he didn't see them everyday.

The door unlocked and opened and Roman turned and

eyed the man with steely eyes and broad shoulders who filled the doorway. He guessed this was Dana McIntyre's security.

"Good morning. I'm Agent Roman Walsh," he said, lifting his badge for inspection. "I'm here to escort Mrs. McIntyre to Seattle."

The man scrutinized his badge for a moment and then appeared satisfied as he stepped aside.

"I'm Curtis, her security. Come in. She's just about ready."

Roman nodded and stepped into the foyer and immediately entered a two-story family room which gave him a view of the upper floor.

"Have a seat," Curtis said. "She'll be right down."

Roman chose an armchair in the corner of the family room that gave him an even better view of the stairs and the landing above. He wanted to get a good look at the woman who was surprisingly a mystery to him. Although he hadn't been directly involved in the case, he'd read her file and discovered that Dana McIntyre was an accountant and chose to continue working at her firm even after her ex-husband won his senatorial race. She had always refused to testify against the Senator while they were married. She had never been legally obligated to, so the FBI had all but left her alone. Now that they were divorced, the bureau obviously had seen their chance and went after her for her shady accounting practices in order to catch the big prize, her ex-husband. Still, there wasn't much to learn about her. The pictures in her file were vague to say the least. He could barely make out a black woman with light complexion, possibly in her late 30's, medium height with dark hair just past her shoulders and a slim build with subtle curves. She didn't seem to cater to the media either, because nearly all of the pictures were of her turning away from the camera or lowering her head.

When Roman heard noise above him signaling feet walking across the landing, he looked up immediately and got his first clear look at the Senator's ex-wife and she was definitely an eye-catcher. She was dressed warm in jeans that hugged her curvy thighs, a sweater that couldn't hide her full breasts and boots that looked great with her legs. She had to have noticed him at the same time, because her footsteps immediately halted, and she looked at him as he stood below her in the family room. Roman's eyes trailed her body once again and then her face and finally his mind registered the familiarity of it all. He knew this woman, those curves that now filled out, those narrowed dark eyes and that subtle smile that tugged at the corners of her lips. He was staring at someone he knew as a young woman. She was fully grown now, and it had to be about fifteen years since he'd seen her at Cal State. Only she hadn't been Dana McIntyre back then. She'd been Dana Corbin. Dana Corbin, his friend and eventually his girlfriend, is the woman he was going to be spending the next day and a half with.

Damn.

CHAPTER THREE

*R*oman Walsh.

She nearly said his name out loud just to hear how it sounded on her lips. He was actually standing there—a man she never thought she'd see again was standing just a few feet away from her. He was tall and ruggedly handsome with the same gray eyes she used to love staring into. He'd always had muscles in college since he played team sports, but add fifteen years, and his build was now imposing.

Roman was her escort to Seattle.

The actions she'd taken had led her to this moment, but in the back of her mind, she always knew something like this would eventually happen. The universe had this weird sense of humor of reuniting a woman with the man whom she had a crush on in high school, who finally paid her some attention in college, dated her, slept with her and then dumped her when his prom queen girlfriend decided to take him back.

A voice cleared and they both turned to see Curtis darting his head between the two of them, curiously.

"You two know each other?"

"Yes," Dana said.

"No," Roman said at the same time.

She widened her eyes at him. "No," she parroted. "Are you sure about that, Roman?"

His jaw tightened. "It's Agent Walsh, and I meant to say we used to know each other. It's been a long time."

Not long enough, apparently, Dana thought to herself.

Roman cleared his throat and made a show of looking at his wristwatch. "Are you ready, Mrs. McIntyre? I'd like to get going."

"I'm ready," she said, tugging along the wheeled suitcase by her side. She descended the stairs, keeping her eyes solely on Roman while he now seemed to be looking everywhere else but at her.

Curtis took her suitcase from her and walked it out to Roman's car. She grabbed her coat and purse and followed them out to a silver SUV parked directly in front of the house. As Curtis put the bags in the trunk, Dana caught a glimpse of several carefully wrapped Christmas presents already nestling neatly inside. She looked to Roman and saw he was staring at her again, but then he instantly looked away and got into the car.

"Thank you, Curtis," she said, shaking her guard's hand. "Merry Christmas to you and your family."

"Merry Christmas to you, too and safe travels. Call me if you need anything," he said, giving her a meaningful look.

"I will," she said, turning to get into the passenger seat.

He held the door open for her and closed it once she was inside. Silence immediately filled the SUV's interior. For the first time in fifteen years, she was alone with Roman Walsh.

She waved goodbye to Curtis as he returned to the townhouse to lock it up for the rest of the week—or for however long this whole thing was going to last.

The plan was to move her to a safe house in Seattle,

which is where the trial against Senator McIntyre would take place. Dana thought again for the millionth time if she was doing the right thing. She'd gone back and forth on her decision so many times. If the critical moment came, she wasn't so sure she'd be able to go through with it. But there were people counting on her, and if she set aside her personal feelings, maybe, just maybe she could see this all the way through.

For now, she simply leaned back in the passenger seat and watched as Roman battled the traffic of last minute holiday shoppers and navigated them through residential neighborhoods where Christmas decorations adorned homes. Deflated snowmen, Disney characters and Santa littered several yards, until that appointed time at dusk when they would fill up with air, lights and music and entertain all those who drove by. She both loved and hated this time of year.

Without appearing too obvious, she slid a sideways glance at Roman. His attention was focused on the road, but he looked to be somewhere else, lost in his thoughts. The news was playing on the car radio, and she got the impression he wasn't really listening to it and only turned it on to drown out the taut silence.

"Who are the presents for?"

"What?" he asked, looking momentarily startled by her voice.

She sat up, hitching a thumb toward the trunk. "The Christmas presents back there. Who are they for?"

"My kids," he grunted.

That surprised her, but as she thought more about it, it sounded just like Roman. Even in his twenties with his sports jock status, he struck her as the family guy type. She just knew he'd get married right after college to a lovely girl from a good family who'd give him a houseful of kids. Sadly, she didn't fit that bill, but maybe it was for the best. For years, marriage and kids had been the furthest thing from Dana's mind. However, now with every birthday that passed, ticking her closer and closer to forty, she was feeling the overpowering need and desire to be a mother.

"Where are they?"

"Back in California with Kyra—I mean, with their mother. After I drop you off, I'm going to leave my car at the airport and get a flight back to San Francisco. That way, I can see them Christmas Eve and Christmas day."

It was too late. He tried to cover it up, but she'd heard and recognized the name. Kyra and Roman had been high school sweethearts, but when graduation came, and they all enrolled in college, she'd set her sights on one of the upperclassmen, leaving Roman broken-hearted. Then, when it was apparent that Roman had moved on, Kyra suddenly wanted a second chance, and he'd been all too willing to give her one, doing to Dana what Kyra had done to him. But that was years ago. This was now, and she couldn't allow those memories to flood back and distract her from the job at hand.

But as she listened to him talk about seeing his kids on Christmas, she couldn't mistake the hope in his voice. Guilt instantly overwhelmed her, and she tried her best to tamp it down.

"What's wrong?" he asked, obviously noticing her sudden uneasiness.

She quickly made up something. "I'm just nervous about the trial."

He nodded and then went silent. A few minutes passed before he spoke again.

"This isn't my case. I was ordered to escort you because the agent in charge of the investigation got held up, so I don't have a dog in this fight." He paused. "Still, I shouldn't be saying this, but I'm going to say it anyway."

"What's that?"

"You don't have to do this." He took his eyes off the road for just a moment to look at her. "I mean testifying against your ex-husband. You don't have to do it if you're having second thoughts. I'm sure your lawyers can get you out of any trouble you might be in."

She let out a self-deprecating laugh. "You're right. I could walk away from all of this. But then there goes my protection. Do you really think the Senator is just going to let me walk away after I cast such a bright spotlight on him?"

He faced the road again and that stiffened jaw returned. "I see you really chose well for yourself, Mrs. McIntyre."

Dana turned a little in her seat and stared at him. She should just let that sarcastic remark go, but couldn't. Just for the fun of it, she wanted to see if she could rattle him in the least.

"I divorced him, didn't I?"

He nodded stiffly. "Before or after you reaped the benefits of his illegal dealings?"

"Well, I guess I make a lot of mistakes when it comes to men."

He looked at her as though he really wanted to say something to that, but instead just shook his head and faced the road again.

"Forget I said anything," he said. "It's your choice. I'm just going to drop you off and get back to my family."

"You mean you're going to dump me again and go back to Kyra?"

His hands tightened on the steering wheel, and she gave herself a mental fist pump. Maybe that remark was childish, but she was so tired of his act. They weren't strangers, no matter how much he wished they were. He'd had a big effect on her, so much so that she'd thought about him off and on over the years. He'd been her first love. Her ego would like to think he felt the same, but more than likely, she was only fooling herself. As soon as he'd gotten what he wanted from her all those years ago and greener pastures came calling, he'd been done with her.

CHAPTER FOUR

California State University, October 2001

"Are you okay?"

Roman came away from his thoughts and looked at Dana who was staring up at him curiously. They had just left a Fraternity party and were walking side by side back to her dorm room.

"I'm good," he lied. "I've just never been much for parties."

"But you play sports," she countered. "I thought all jocks loved parties."

"Not this jock," he said, crooking a half-smile.

"Well, sorry, I just thought you could use a night out. We've been studying a lot, and I appreciate you tutoring me for my history mid-term."

"So, you thank me by taking me to a frat party?"

She stopped and punched him in the arm playfully. "Hey, I'm in college. I have limited options."

"You said your roommate was away visiting her parents for the weekend. You could've invited me over for all that home cooking you keep bragging about."

Dana laughed as they resumed walking. "When I get paid

from my job, I can go grocery shopping and make you something in the common area."

"I'll buy the groceries," he offered. "Just go with me and get what you need."

"You don't have to do that," she said.

"I want to. Please," he said, putting his hands in the prayer position. "I'm desperate to eat something else besides cafeteria food or noodles."

"Aww, poor baby," she said in a sweet, mocking tone. "I have some leftovers from the last time I made my roommate and I dinner. I can give you some to tide you over until then."

"You had me at leftovers."

She laughed and then the humor slowly faded as she got lost in her own thoughts. "Are you sure you want to come up?"

"Sure," he said. "It's a coed dorm and visiting hours haven't ended yet. Why do you ask?"

"No, I mean…" She stopped walking again and looked at him with all seriousness. "I saw Kyra at the party with her new boyfriend, and I know you saw her, too."

He shrugged. "So?"

"Come on, Roman. I know she means a lot to you—"

"*Meant*," he said, firmly. "She *meant* a lot to me. That's all over now."

"Is it?"

"Yes. She made her choice. There's nothing between us anymore."

"Then why do you look so sad?"

He paused, looked away for a moment and then cursed under his breath. "Okay. I'll admit it sucks seeing her with another guy—an older guy. But I can't forget how as soon as high school was over, she was done with me. I need to be done with her, too."

Dana cocked her head to one side and frowned. "So, is

that why I'm standing here with you? You want me to help you be done with her?"

He stepped closer to her and brushed the back of his hand down her arm, loving how soft she felt, dying to know if the rest of her was just as soft. In fact, he'd been dying to know all through high school, but since he'd fallen so hard for Kyra, he didn't want to mess things up. Still, when he caught Dana waving and smiling at him between classes or at lunch, he wondered how it would be if she were his. Too often when he was alone at night in his room, it wasn't Kyra who came to his mind.

He cupped both of his hands to Dana's face and brought his lips down to kiss her. It was a warm and sweet-tasting kiss. He sucked gently at her full lips just like he did to her in his fantasies, and she immediately opened her mouth to accept him greedily. Her arms came around his neck, and he indulged himself just a little longer before he forced himself to stay back. They would soon be drawing a crowd, and that's not what he wanted. He wanted Dana Corbin all to himself.

"Wow," she said, breathlessly. "What took you so long to do that?"

He smiled, took her hand in his and continued on to her dorm. "I guess I was distracted."

CHAPTER FIVE

"I don't know what to tell you, Roman. The kids will be visiting my parents on Christmas day. My brothers and sisters will be there, too, and it will be good for Tyler and Brianna to see their cousins."

Roman used to envy Kyra for coming from a large family. She had her two parents and four other brothers and sisters who all had at least two children of their own. Holidays, especially Christmas, were always an event, and he used to look forward to them every year. His parents were enjoying retirement in Florida, and his brother lived in Phoenix, so Christmas consisted of phone calls and presents that were mailed. He wasn't ungrateful at all, but there was something about a big family during the holidays that made it all the more special. But now, that big family of Kyra's was interfering with his time with his kids.

"You know I was supposed to have them Christmas day. We agreed this year they would spend the day with me—not at your parents'."

"I know, but when you called and told me you had to

escort a witness to Washington, I went ahead and changed plans." She paused and sighed. "This isn't the first time you cancelled on them because something came up at work. I didn't want them to be disappointed again."

He shut his eyes, pinching the bridge of his nose and tried to resist the temptation to throw the phone across the wall.

"Kyra, don't do this. I miss them."

"Then come to my parents' house. They'd love to see you —everyone would."

His temper flared. "Oh yeah? Would Scott love to see me, too? Because I can guarantee you if I see him, it won't be a merry fucking Christmas."

"Roman, stop! Look, I'm not doing this with you. Brianna and Tyler will be with us at their grandparent's house on Christmas. You can come or not. It's up to you."

He should have just stopped, counted to ten then twenty and taken several deep breaths. Perhaps if he was calmer, he could get her to relent somehow. But he couldn't get past what she'd just said: 'The kids will be with *us*'.

Us. Such a simple word with a lot of hidden meaning and to him it meant pain and betrayal. *Us* used to mean the two of them, and now it meant her and someone else—with his kids.

He spoke in an even tone laced with anger. "Tell me, what world do you live in where it's perfectly fine that the man you cheated on me with gets to see my kids more than me?"

She hung up.

When he heard the signal that the call had ended, he tossed the phone to the side, sat back against the headboard of his bed and turned on the TV, hoping the white noise would calm his anger. Several hours into the trip, it had begun to grow dark and he became hungry. It was scheduled in the trip to take an overnight rest break, and Dana didn't object. So, he pulled into a motel somewhere near the border of California and Washington and got them two connected rooms with a shared bath.

His conversation with Kyra was just further proof that he needed to take her to court and get an amended custody agreement. As much as it went against his morals, he needed that money. He just had to take Dana on a slight detour, collect the other half of it and start looking for a lawyer.

Still, in the back of his mind, he couldn't shake the fact that this was all too good to be true and that he should've just walked away when he was approached with this deal. He never thought he'd be an agent who was on the take—not like his ex-partner, Harry.

Roman used to judge and criticize him when he found out what he was up to and swore he'd never be the same. Now if Harry could only see him now. He'd laugh and ridicule Roman for being on his high horse and judging him when all it took were the right set of circumstances to make him a dirty fed, too.

But even with all of that, he had to find a way to continue on, because it was for Brianna and Tyler's sake. For them, he could find a way to put his conscience aside and do what needed to be done. And yet, there was another part of this equation he hadn't expected—the senator's wife was not just some faceless, nameless woman. She was Dana.

Sitting next to her in the car for several hours had been agonizing. All he wanted to do was look at her and marvel at how the years had been good to her. She'd been his girlfriend for only a few months, but those few months had left an impression on him that he'd been unable to shake for years. Dana had been something special, and it was a shame he never let her know that. He chose to treat her like a secret, when she was anything but that, and he just couldn't understand why. Ironic, how all these years later, the woman he thought was perfect for him once again chose someone over him, and the woman he discarded was now literally by his side.

But that was all in the past. She might've been what he wanted back in college, but she wasn't that girl anymore. She was a woman who made the decision to marry a corrupt politician, reap the benefits of that corruption by cooking his books for him and then exact revenge after it all ended. The sad truth was, he didn't know her anymore and wasn't too sure he wanted to get to know her again.

Thinking about her now, he looked to the closed door of the adjoining room and turned the volume down on the TV. He listened, but no sound came from the other room. He got up from the bed, crossed to the closed door and knocked.

"Mrs. McIntyre?"

No answer.

He tried again, but when he was still met with silence, he twisted the knob. The door swung open easily, and he peeked his head in and looked around. His eyes went to the bed first in case she was sleeping, but the covers were undisturbed. He looked around the rest of the room and saw it was empty.

The law enforcement officer in him told him not to panic just yet. She could've gone for a walk and he wouldn't have heard her leave while arguing with Kyra. But before he went to the front door, he noticed the closed door to the bathroom they shared. He walked over, raised his hand to knock and then paused. He could hear her in there, and it sounded like she was talking to someone.

"We stopped at a motel for the night...Yes, I'm fine. I'll call if anything changes. Is everything still a go? Don't worry about me. I'll do my part. I need to go. All right, talk soon."

Seeing red, Roman shoved open the door, and she

whirled around with wide eyes. He was ready to spit fire, but the man inside of him brought his movements to a halt when he saw she was standing there fresh out of the shower with a towel wrapped around her still damp body.

Yes, he did remember her, but his memories didn't do her any justice.

CHAPTER SIX

"Give it to me," Roman demanded, his hand outstretched.

Dana tucked the phone behind her back. "I can have a phone, Agent Walsh."

"No, you can't," he said and snaked an arm around her waist and brought her back to his front while keeping her arms immobile.

"What are you doing?" she asked, struggling against him.

"Hold still," he said, trying to wrench the phone free but she was twisting and turning trying to keep it away from him.

She strained against him, but he succeeded in finally prying the phone out of her hands. By the time he released her, they were both breathing heavily, her hair had come undone and was tumbling down in dark waves across her face. Her light brown skin was flushed and her eyes were wide with shock.

"What the hell?" she asked, panting and with each breath her breasts heaved up and down, dangerously close to being released from the towel.

He didn't know why, but suddenly he couldn't control his hands. He stepped forward and reached out to tug the towel back in place, but she moved to secure it before he did and now she was looking at him curiously.

"I got it," she said.

He nodded, stepping back. "Of course. Sorry."

"So, do you want to tell me what that was all about?"

"Why don't you tell me who you were just talking to," he countered, slipping the phone he'd just confiscated into his back jeans pocket.

"My security, Curtis. He asked me to check in to assure him I'm safe."

"You asked him if everything was still a go and you said you'd do your part. What was that about?"

She heaved a sigh. "He wanted to buy his daughter a big dollhouse for Christmas but they were all sold out. I have a friend who works in the corporate offices of one of the big toy companies. She said she'd get one out to him. It's supposed to be a surprise, and I wanted to make sure he'd be home in time for the delivery. That's all."

He studied her for a moment and saw something devious in her eyes. She was hiding something from him, but he didn't have the desire to guess at it. Let her have her secrets, because he just wanted this trip over with. Tomorrow couldn't come soon enough.

"Listen to me, Mrs. McIntyre. That was the first and last call you'll make. From now on, if you need to contact someone, let me know, and we use my phone."

She nodded, and they continued to stare at one another. He really should leave, but he was too busy reacquainting his mind with the memory of how she looked under that towel and how good she felt in his arms.

"Is that all or is there something else you want to take from me?" she asked.

He caught the double meaning, but instead of taking her up on that offer, he began to back out of the bathroom. "Get dressed. There's a diner next door, and I'm starving."

* * *

Dana's eyes slowly trailed above the menu to stare at the top of Roman's head. Her mind was still preoccupied with the way he'd stared at her inside the bathroom. The last time she'd seen that lustful look in his eyes, she was twenty-one. But they weren't in their 20's anymore. They were in their late 30's, two fully grown consenting adults. So, when he looked at her as if he wanted to snatch off her towel, she stared right back, urging him to go ahead. Then her senses kicked in. He was an FBI agent escorting her to a safe house. This was a job—not a booty call. But that lingering thought of 'what if' still plagued her. Despite her old wounds from his dismissal of her years ago, she wanted to see and feel if he was still the tender and passionate guy he'd been back then. Something told her he was more.

Soon, the server came to take their drink and food orders, and they were both forced to give up the large menus that had served as invisible barriers between them.

Dana cleared her throat. "Earlier, I was going to knock on your door to ask if you wanted to use the bathroom before I did, but I heard you on the phone. You sounded upset. Everything okay?"

He looked at her as if he were going to tell her to mind her own business, but then he looked away, watching the other patrons in the diner. His mind seemed to be burdened with thoughts and when he faced her again, she saw relief in his eyes. He wanted to talk to someone.

"Kyra, my ex-wife, won't let me have my kids on Christmas."

"Ex-wife? You two are divorced?"

He nodded. "Yes. Why? Do you want to say 'I told you so'?"

She frowned. As bright of a torch he carried for Kyra in high school and college, she'd always expected their marriage to last.

"No, I don't, and I'm sorry to hear that. Did she say why she won't let you have the kids?"

He sighed and thanked the server when she brought them their drinks and continued.

"As you can imagine, my job can be demanding. I work a lot of hours, and there have been times—many times where I've had to cancel plans on my kids. I hated myself every time for it, but I always left it up to her to explain it to them for me. I never had to see their disappointed looks or tears. I guess she got tired of it and decided this time, Christmas would be on her terms. She's taking them to her parents' home."

"Are you welcome there?"

"Yeah, but that's not the point. I wanted them with me."

She shrugged. "I get it, but take it from someone who grew up without a dad. They'll appreciate it more if they see you Christmas day. They won't care where it is. They just want to see you and spend time with you."

By the time their food arrived, he was still frowning, and she knew he wasn't satisfied at all. He obviously loved his children and wanted them all to himself for the holiday. It was hard for him to adjust to the fact that he now had to share their time and attention, and an unwanted feeling of compassion for him rose up in her. But, she couldn't afford to feel this way, not when she had a job to do.

"What about your family?" he asked.

"What about them?" Dana asked, unwrapping her straw and placing it into her drink.

"It doesn't sound very festive to be spending your Christmas in FBI custody. How's your mom doing? I'm sure she would like to see you."

She smiled. "Ah, so you do remember me, and it hasn't been too long that you forgot details of my life."

"I guess not," he said, cutting into his steak and eggs.

"Anything else you remember about our college days?"

He shrugged one shoulder and forked a piece of steak into his mouth. "Just the fact that we dated a few months and then moved on. What else is there to remember?"

She smirked, masking the fact that it hurt her for him to be so dismissive of memories that she still felt were very special.

"What else is there to remember? Well, how about those days when it rained and we'd drive somewhere secluded to make out in your car. You said you liked the sound of the rain mixed with the sounds of us both coming."

He stopped chewing his food, and it seemed his entire body stilled as he slowly raised his eyes to look at her.

Dana stared right back. "Do you remember how I'd make you dinner, we'd sit and laugh about the dumbest things and talk about what we wanted to do with our lives after college?"

"What are you doing?" he asked.

But she ignored him and kept reminiscing. "How about the days when we'd study in the library together. There were subjects you'd tutor me in and subjects I'd tutor you in. But after all that studying, we found a dark quiet corner between all the shelves of old books and then dare each other to keep quiet while you dove under my blouse...or skirt."

"I'm not here for this, Dana."

"Yes. Dana. That's my name. Not Mrs. McIntyre. Dana!"

She looked at him for a long time, as memories, both sensual and sweet, flooded her mind, too. She'd done it to aggravate him, pissed that he would treat their history as nothing more than a bump in the road. But her punishment had only backfired, because with the onslaught of memories, she realized with a pang of sadness just how much she enjoyed every waking minute of those days and just how much she had missed him over the years.

She stood abruptly from the table. "I need to use the restroom. By the way, my mom is doing good. I'll call her on Christmas and visit her after the holidays when all of this is over. Thanks for asking."

As soon as they returned from the diner, she locked herself in the bathroom once again, but this time, he was going to wait for her. He went into her room, listened as she ran the faucet water and then there was quiet. Still, he waited, not at all about to let her get away with what she'd just pulled.

When she finally opened the door that connected to her bedroom, he greeted her by immediately pushing her back into the bathroom and slamming the door shut behind him. He walked her backwards until her back was against the nearest wall and leaned in close to her face.

"Let me explain something to you," he hissed. "I'm just here to do a job—not play memory lane with you. You're a paycheck to me, that's it. I'm going to drop you at your new temporary home and you're free to air your ex-husband's dirty laundry as much as you want while saving your own ass. But I'm going home to see my kids. That's the plan, and I don't want to hear anything more out of you about anything else but that plan. Got it?"

"Back off of me," she warned.

But with all that bark, he was enjoying the position they were in. As much as it irritated him to have her talk so candidly about their memories, the whole thing still turned him on and left him wanting to relive all of it.

He moved in even closer, so close that their bodies were practically touching, and it had been a long time since he'd had any woman besides Kyra this close to him.

"Is that what you really want me to do?"

He got a good look at her and read the anger in her eyes. But there was something else there, too. He was crowding her, and he remembered just how much she liked it. She was turned on, too..

"To answer your question, I remember everything," he said. "More than you know. But you know what I especially remember? Valentine's Day. You remember what happened after we left the drive-in and went to your dorm room?"

She nodded slowly, and her mouth parted ever so slightly. Watching every movement, he couldn't help but put two fingers to her lips and felt the moistness. In answer, she stuck out her tongue to lick his fingers, and he inhaled sharply as the pleasure went straight to his jeans where he was throbbing for her.

"Show me what you remember," he said, barely keeping it together.

She seemed to be hesitating.

"Go ahead and show me," he urged. "Let's get it out of our systems, and then we can get back to work."

Defiance filled her eyes, which he knew it would. He was betting on it. She lightly licked his index and middle fingers one more time and keeping her eyes on him, she took that same hand and guided it down to the waistband of her slacks. She then pulled at the elastic and shoved his hand down her pants and inside her panties. There, he allowed his fingers to graze across the smoothness of her skin. She was bare and wet down there, all primed and ready to grant his fingers access.

He braced his free hand on the bathroom wall just above her head and bore his eyes into hers. "Ready?"

She spread her legs, gripped the back of his neck and pulled him down closer to whisper in his ear.

"Do it."

He plunged two fingers into her and watched with delight as she squirmed. He stroked them in and out of her and Jesus, she was so wet. He took his fingers, spread that hot center of her apart and put his thumb directly on the tiny bud and rubbed slowly.

"Roman!"

She shut her eyes tight to the oncoming pleasure, but he wanted to see her. He wanted to see that moment when she surrendered and completely belong to him.

"Open your eyes. Look at me."

She did so, and he stared at her as he increased the pressure and the speed of his caress. Her hands were still gripping the back of his neck for balance, but her nails were now biting into his skin as she whimpered and moaned his name. She moved her hips in time to his fingers, and he rubbed his thumb faster and faster, watching with awe as she got closer to the brink, ready to explode. Finally, she opened her mouth and her cry of unabashed pleasure seemed to go on and on.

She always knew how to make his ego soar.

CHAPTER EIGHT

Friday, December 24th

The next morning, they exchanged about ten words between each other as they packed up their few belongings and checked out of the motel. The drive was even more awkward and silent than the previous day, and the only thing that stopped Roman from going out of his mind was the Christmas music station on the radio and the fact that Dana seemed to be preoccupied with the snow blanketing the roads, pine trees and homes they passed. It all seemed to put her in good spirits.

He, himself, had never used to be a fan of Christmas, but when he and Kyra started a family, he came to look forward to the looks of joy and wide-eyed wonder on his children's faces whenever they saw the house lit up, the tree decorated and the tons of presents that came under that tree. Not to mention, Kyra had Christmas music playing non-stop. Many times, decorating and baking came to halt in favor of *Santa Claus is Coming to Town*. But those days had passed. Now, he had to figure out how he was going to make his own Christmas memories with his kids.

He looked over at Dana who had that same look of inno-cent joy Brianna and Tyler had, and he suddenly and surpris-ingly wished he could do something for her to make it last.

"There's a rest stop coming up," she said, pointing at a sign on the road. "You need gas, and I want to get a snack."

He nodded and took the exit for the rest stop. The first thing he noticed was a crowd of people walking up and down what looked to be the town's main street. Adults and kids alike were standing around, smiling, laughing and talking excitedly.

"It looks like a parade is about to start," Dana said.

He looked over at her again and couldn't help but crack a smile at the way she seemed to elevate in her seat from the anticipation of it all. When they stopped at the station, he got out and began to pump the gas. She got out, too and turned to him.

"Can I get you anything?"

He shook his head and continued to watch her as she entered the convenience store. Even bundled up in a winter coat, he could see just how delectable that figure of hers was. Just like that, his thoughts went to last night and how she completely came apart in front of him. That encounter would stay with him forever. He didn't even know what came over him, because seducing her had been the furthest thing from his mind. But it was as if all he needed was to set eyes on her again, and all the memories, the emotions, every-thing he felt for her back in college came rushing back, and he couldn't bear to not touch her.

After she came all over his hand, he stepped back, helped her right her clothes and watched with fascination as she steadied her breathing. Then it was as if neither of them knew what to say or do with each other.

"I—I really need to get to bed," she said. "We're leaving early, right?"

He nodded. "Yeah. Goodnight."

But he couldn't sleep. Not with a hard-on that was begging for her and only her. As soon as she closed the door to her bedroom, he used the shower and rubbed himself down, pretending it was her hands on him.

"Roman?"

He broke away from his erotic thoughts to find her standing on the other side of the car with her arms loaded down with snacks.

"What?"

"I said you're missing the parade."

She gestured behind him, and he turned to see that the Christmas festivities had begun. He replaced the gas pump and smiled at the many colorful floats of elves, reindeer and ice princesses that trailed slowly down the street. All the characters waved enthusiastically to the crowd, tossing candy canes and shouting out holiday cheer. All of it eventually led up to the main attraction of Santa and Mrs. Claus.

"Do you take your kids to Christmas parades," Dana asked, coming to stand beside him.

"I would like to, but their mother has more time for that than I do. Whenever I get them during the holidays, I take them through different neighborhoods at night to see the houses lit up. They like that."

She smiled. "It's just my mom and I, but I love doing that, too."

He took his eyes off the floats and looked at her. "I remember."

They stared at each other for a long time and he felt something special pass between them. Something like a shared bond.

She cleared her throat. "Can I see a picture of your kids?"

He took out his phone and scrolled through his gallery until he came to their pictures and handed the phone to her.

While she cooed over them, he noticed a dark sedan parked several yards away. Two men he didn't recognize were sitting inside and they looked to be staring at them. Could these be Senator McIntyre's men, waiting for him to pick up his money and then lead them to safe house? A feeling of foreboding came over him, but he'd already come this far.

"We should get going," he said, taking his phone back. "I don't want to get behind schedule."

CHAPTER NINE

*R*oman drove the SUV up the snow plowed path and followed the road until they came to a house that looked abandoned. He shut off the ignition, looked around the dense woods surrounding them and up at the house again. Fresh snow had fallen on the rooftop and along the porch railing and steps. It was completely undisturbed and looked like one of those magical cottages he would read about in Brianna's bedtime stories.

"Are you sure this is it?" Dana asked, also peering about. "I thought the safe house was closer to Seattle. We're still about three hours away."

"I was told to stop here for further instructions," he lied. "For security reasons, your final location was withheld. Stay here. Let me go in and check things out."

He started to get out of the car, but she grabbed the sleeve of his coat, halting him.

"Roman, wait."

He turned back to look at her.

"I'm going to tell you the same thing you told me: You don't have to do this."

"What do you mean?" he asked, frowning.

"I mean we can just drive away. Let's go find a nice restaurant, have an early Christmas dinner and then part ways."

He chuckled. "What are you talking about? You're supposed to be testifying. You're in FBI custody."

"Am I?" she asked, and she was giving him an odd look. "Am I in FBI custody right now?"

"Of course. You're with me. Look, let me go inside. My final instructions should be in there, and then we can go. We can't just stay here. We'll catch cold out here in the snow."

"Roman," she pleaded, but in answer, he tugged his arm free, got out and shut the door.

He wondered where all that came from. Why did she suddenly want to walk away from all of this? Why did she want him to? He was going inside to get his money, see her safely transferred out of his hands and then go give his kids their Christmas presents. This was almost over, and he couldn't let Dana sidetrack him now.

* * *

As soon as he disappeared through the front door of the house, Dana cursed him and herself for what she now had to do. She pulled out the second phone she'd kept hidden in her purse, scrolled through her contacts and dialed a number.

"Dana, is that you?" Alex asked, sounding frantic.

"Yeah, it's me."

"Christ, I've been worried. What happened?"

"He heard me on the phone talking to you and took my other phone. I almost blew my cover then, so I couldn't risk calling again. But we're here. Walsh just went inside the house."

"Good. Follow him inside. I need you to witness him taking the money."

She looked around once again, suddenly feeling uneasy. "Alex, what is this place? Why did you tell him to come here?"

"I need another agent to witness him taking the bribe. It will hold up better in court. After you make the arrest, backup will be there to take him into custody, and you can continue on to deliver that list."

An ache went straight to her heart. She'd tried to get Roman to stop what he was about to do. She didn't want to go in there and arrest him, but this was her job, and he'd made his choice.

Dammit! Why did they have to have that sexual moment last night? Why did she have to ask to see pictures of his kids? She knew this was coming and had tried so hard to mentally prepare herself for every outcome. She just didn't prepare herself for Roman or what it would do to her seeing him again after so long.

"Dana?"

"Yes, okay. I'm going in. When does backup get here?"

"I'm dispatching Adams and Russo now. They'll be there in twenty minutes."

"Right." She hung up the phone and reached in her bag for something else she'd hidden there—her badge and service revolver. She then got out of the car and crept toward the house.

CHAPTER TEN

Roman entered the vacant house and moved through the first floor cautiously. He was inside what used to be a small living area. A fireplace was on his left and an open door that led to an underground cellar was on his right. He continued on toward the kitchen, following the instructions he'd committed to memory. Inside the abandoned kitchen, he crossed to the refrigerator and shoved it aside. Roaches scurried away, and he put his weight on one of the floorboards. It rocked back and forth. He knelt down and used his hands to pry the loose board away. He then shone his pocket flashlight inside the hole and saw a small wrapped bundle. He reached in, grabbed it and eagerly unwrapped it to find a padded envelope similar to the one he'd gotten that night inside the parking garage. He peered inside and drew out two bundles of money rubber banded together.

Counting the amount in his head, he felt disgusted with himself. He tried to picture Brianna and Tyler, but this time even their innocent faces weren't enough to make him feel good about what he was doing. He was selling out a witness, he was selling out Dana. Sure, she must have done something illegal to warrant a deal with the FBI, but it didn't excuse what he was doing, nor did it erase how he felt about her.

The Senator's men were no doubt close by, waiting for them to leave and for him to lead them to the real safe house where they would intercept Dana. And then what? Did he really think he would just be able to walk away with the money, leaving her alone to those men?

"Fuck!" He expelled.

He couldn't do this—not to her, not to anyone. He wasn't sure what his plan was, but he knew they were getting out of here. He wasn't going to hand her to the wolves.

With the money still clutched in his hand, he stood and kicked the floorboard back into place. That's when he heard her soft voice behind him, and it was rife with warning.

"Drop it, Agent Walsh. Put your hands up and slowly turn around."

He dropped the envelope of money, and it landed to the floor with an incriminating thud. He then slowly put his hands up and turned to face her. A gun was aimed at his chest, held by the woman he so desperately wanted a second encounter with. But that stolen intimate moment of last night was the furthest thing from his mind as anger and confusion washed over him in waves.

"What is this?" he asked, even though his instincts were already telling him.

"I'm Agent Dana Corbin with Internal Affairs, and I'm hereby placing you under arrest for charges of bribery and conspiracy."

CHAPTER ELEVEN

California State University, February 2002

"You're surprising me with how romantic you are."

"What do you mean?" Roman asked, snuggling her closer to him in the back seat of his car.

"Dinner and a drive-in theater on Valentine's Day," Dana said, smiling. "Not bad for a college student."

He shrugged, smiling. "I can turn on the charm when I want. I appreciate you letting me pick the movie. I really didn't want to sit through a romantic comedy."

"I like action movies, too," she said, grabbing a fistful of popcorn and attempting to stuff it all into her mouth.

Roman laughed as only a few of the kernels made it inside her mouth, while the rest went all over the back seat.

"I guess I know where you'll be tomorrow—at the car wash vacuuming this stuff up."

She looked up at him and whispered into his ear. "Something tells me you're going to let it slide."

"Am I?"

She nodded, slyly. "My roommate is at her boyfriend's tonight, so you and I have the dorm room all to ourselves."

His eyes widened in surprise. He had to admit the very thought excited him. With both of them living on campus, it had been hard finding a place to go where they could be alone. Hotels got expensive and so most nights, they hung out in the student union hall with so many other kids, grabbed some comfortable chairs in the back and sat there talking or kissing for hours. At some point, someone would yell for them to get a room, to which Roman would flip them the bird.

"We would if we could instead of sitting here with you assholes!" He'd say, making Dana both giggle and cringe from embarrassment.

So, the prospect of having an entire dorm room all to themselves for the night was akin to winning the lottery.

"When does she leave?" he asked, eagerly.

Dana laughed and kissed him on the cheek. "Watch the movie. We have plenty of time."

He tried to put his attention back on the action flick, but curiosity had him looking at the other cars around them, and when he saw who was in the car right next to theirs, he suddenly wished he hadn't brought Dana here.

Kyra, sitting next to her boyfriend, noticed him at the same time he noticed her. She seemed to be focused on his arms wrapped around Dana's shoulders with her head lounging against his chest, and Roman for some reason had the dumbest urge to explain himself to her.

Finally, Kyra's eyes met his again and she smiled and shyly waved. He waved back and when he looked over at Dana, he knew she had seen the entire exchange.

"Maybe we should go," she said. "It's getting crowded here, and we can have movie night in my room."

Roman was both relieved and angry, but at himself. This

night was supposed to be for her, and it had been cut short because of his uneasiness.

He pulled away from the drive-in, and the entire ride back to her dorm, they chatted about everything else except seeing Kyra. It was as if Dana wanted to pretend it didn't happen, and he was willing to oblige her. Still, he wanted to make it up to her, and having her all too himself would allow him to do just that.

By the time they got to her room, they were laughing and full of excitement.

"I hope you plan to take advantage of me," she said. "There's no telling when this is going to happen again."

"Believe me, I'm taking advantage of you," he promised.

She opened the door to her room, gave a little squeal of happiness to find it empty and pulled him inside.

"Oh yeah? What do you have in mind?"

He shut the door behind him and turned around to wink at her. "You'll see."

CHAPTER TWELVE

She'd found two old rickety chairs in the house, sat him down in one and cuffed his hands behind his back and then sat down in the other facing him with her gun resting on her lap. They'd been that way for ten minutes. Every now and then, she'd look his way only to find him staring back at her with repressed fury. After the third time she caught him looking at her that way, she'd had enough.

"You have the nerve to be pissed at me? You're on the take, Agent Walsh. Did you really think you would get away with this?"

"Where is the real Mrs. McIntyre?"

She sighed, realizing she should have known he would never admit to guilt.

"She was escorted to her safe house days ago. Alex Bailey, one of the senior agents in my department was convinced you we're accepting bribes just like your ex-partner. He's the one you met in the parking garage that night. He brought me in to play the Senator's wife, because I have a similar liking and build to her. He wanted to see if you would give up my location for a payout." She paused, feeling her own anger now rising at his greed and stupidity. "And you didn't disappoint."

"You can kill the judgmental look," he said. "I know it well. I've used it myself many times."

"Why would you risk your career for that money?" she asked. "You…you were never that way, Roman."

"All I'm going to say is that everything I do, I do for my kids."

She guessed as much, and there went that unwanted feeling of compassion again.

"There are other ways," she said. "Ways that wouldn't land their father in jail or booted out of the agency."

"You're not getting any more out of me until I see a lawyer."

She looked at him now with regret. "Fine, but for what it's worth, it was all just a cover. I didn't use my Finance degree for anything illegal. It just helped me get into the bureau."

"Great," he said. "So, you're not a thief. You're just a liar."

Dana stood from the chair with her gun clutched in her hand, giving him her back as she went to the window and in effect, reconstructing the wall between them.

She looked out the dingy window, but didn't see anything or anyone out there. She checked the time on her phone and saw that nearly twenty minutes had passed. Where was her backup?

"Shouldn't someone be here by now?" Roman asked, guessing at her thoughts.

She didn't answer, but silently admitted to herself that something wasn't right. She scrolled through her contacts to call Alex. His phone rang and rang and eventually, his voice-mail picked up. She frowned, ended the call and started to dial again when a movement outside stopped her. She looked up and saw a nondescript black sedan pull up beside Roman's SUV. There were two men inside, and she didn't recognize either one of them as Agents from IAB.

She looked across the room at Roman who immediately detected the apprehension in her eyes.

"What is it?"

"I don't know."

She called Alex again and his voicemail answered.

"Alex, it's Dana. Call me back as soon as you can. I thought you were sending Adams and Russo. I don't know these—"

The entire room exploded in gunfire, bringing her conversation to a dead halt. Dana reacted instantly and dove for Roman, knocking both him and the chair over. As shots fired all around them, she frantically used her keys to uncuff him. As soon as he was free, she reached in her back waist, tossed him his gun and they both belly-crawled to a corner in the living room away from the firing automatic rounds. There, they remained crouched with their weapons drawn, waiting for the men to stop shooting and come inspect the damage.

The shooting finally ceased, but they kept still in the corner with glass from shattered windows and splintered wood surrounding them. Dana listened for footsteps coming up the walkway, but couldn't hear anything. She turned to Roman, silently asking him what he heard, but he shook his head and kept his eyes and gun trained on the front door.

Another minute went by and Dana was ready to chance a look, when something small and heavy came sailing through the window. By the time she realized what it was, Roman had grabbed her hand, pulled her to the open cellar door and shoved her through. Just as he slammed the door shut behind him, a huge explosion sounded, and the blast from the grenade sent him crashing down the stairs. Dana had managed to take cover under a wooden table, but when she saw him tumble down the stairs, she let out a cry, crawled from under the table and dragged him by the shoulders back to cover. She then shielded his body with her own as the entire house shook and rumbled above them.

CHAPTER THIRTEEN

They stayed in that cellar for a long time until Dana was satisfied the men were gone.

"Are you hurt?" she asked, leaning over Roman and inspecting him for any open wounds.

"I'm fine," he grunted, trying to sit up. "Just sore from that fall. We need to go. We might be in a remote part of the state, but that explosion is going to attract attention."

She agreed and rose to help him to his feet. They found a door in the cellar that led up a short flight of stairs and then outside to the rear of the home. As soon as they emerged from the cellar doors, Dana turned and marveled at the flames, smoke and destruction all around them, and realized that if it hadn't been for Roman's quick thinking, she would be dead. They came around to the front of the house and saw that his SUV was thankfully, still in place. Although it had damage from the debris of the explosion, it was still drivable. Dana tucked Roman into the passenger seat and she ran around to the other side, got in, turned the ignition and got them out of there, fast.

She'd driven for nearly an hour until she found another motor lodge as far from the cabin as possible, booked them a room with cash and helped Roman inside. She treated a minor head wound he had and some scratches of her own with alcohol and bandages she picked up from a drug store. Lastly, he stood and allowed her to remove his t-shirt and inspect for wounds on his chest. She pressed down gently on different pressure points of his bare, muscled chest and looked up at him.

"Nothing seems broken," she said.

He didn't say anything at all, but kept his eyes laser focused on her. Together, they stood there beside the bed, both knowing there was so much that had to be said, but neither of them having either the energy or the courage to speak about what happened and what they were going to do about it.

"I can wrap some bandage around your torso, just in case it's sprained," she continued. "When you fall asleep, the bandages will keep you from moving around and—"

"Shut up," he said, and bent his head low to kiss her open mouth. As he covered her lips with his, he roamed his hands down her lower back and gripped her ass. She felt him hard and straining inside his jeans and the feeling excited her. She pushed herself against him and wrapped her arms around his neck to pull him deeper into her mouth, allowing him to taste and ravage her to his fill. She wanted him on the bed. She wanted to straddle him and have him fill her. She wanted to ride him and make her come until she forgot about every-thing that happened in the last 24 hours. She just wanted to begin again, right here with just the two of them. No painful memories, no bribery, no explosion, no lies.

But the moment she felt him stick his hand into her back pocket and retrieve her cell phone, she knew she'd been fooled once again. He'd been too quick this time, taking advantage of her desire for him. By the time, she backed up and realized what he was doing, he already threw the phone to the ground and smashed it with the heel of his shoe.

"I think it's time you face facts, Agent Corbin," he said, all traces of the earlier lust gone from his voice. "Those men didn't come for me. Someone wants you dead."

* * *

She didn't say anything, but stepped around him, looking ready to spit fire, stalked to the bathroom and slammed the door. The next thing he heard was the shower running, so he donned his t-shirt, grabbed his gun and went out to the car to retrieve their luggage. He was still feeling sore, but he needed to keep moving around. He wasn't tired, he was too wired up and looking for answers. She might be in denial about what just happened at that house, but he was seeing things clearly. For all he could surmise, there was no reason anyone would be after him. He was apart of her sting operation—he'd been brought on this job as a setup, and like a sucker, he fell for it. But that would only lead to his arrest and the eventual loss of his career. Killing him would be unnecessary. Dana was the key. She knew something. Something dangerous enough that her own people, were turning on her.

He pulled their suitcases out of the trunk, looked forlornly at the Christmas presents for his children and then promptly slammed the door. He looked around the parking lot to ensure there were no suspicious vehicles waiting or unfamiliar faces watching him. He went back inside, satisfied they were temporarily out of danger. As he dragged the suitcases back into the room, he saw the bathroom door crack open. She peeked her head out and already had her gun drawn. Maybe she wasn't as in denial as he'd thought.

"It's just me," he said, gesturing to her suitcase. "I brought your clothes inside."

Without a word, she stuck her hand out and he rolled the suitcase over to her. She grabbed the handle, wheeled it inside the bathroom and slammed the door shut again.

"You're welcome," he mumbled, and tossed his duffel bag onto the bed where he rummaged through it until he found his second gun and an extra clip. He tucked the clip in the back of his jeans and sat down in an armchair to wait for Dana to come out of the bathroom.

He knew she was smarting over that kiss, but he didn't have the time or patience to soothe her feelings right now. Yeah, it was a dirty trick, but he needed to get that phone away from her and destroy it. It was a danger to both of them. He thought he'd already taken care of the phone issue, but leave it to a federal agent to have a backup. But as much as that kiss had been a ploy to get what he needed from her, he'd be lying if he said he didn't relish her mouth moving over his or her body melting so easily into him. She'd begun moving her waist in a circular rhythm, rubbing against him and silently begging him for what she needed, and damn him, he really wanted to give it to her. He wanted to get lost inside of her—the woman who'd just arrested him for bribery and conspiracy. Did she forget about that for a moment while she was moaning into his mouth, or like him, did she just not care?

Roman rubbed his hands over his face. With every moment that passed being in her presence, he became more and more tempted to show her just how much of a man he'd become in all these years without her.

Fifteen minutes later, she emerged from the bathroom, showered and changed with her own gun and clip now holstered to her chest. She then began to pace the small room.

"I'm sure you smashed your phone too," she said.

He nodded.

"Then we'll just have to use the phone at the front desk."

He shook his head. "Out of the question. Don't force me to handcuff you to a chair."

She stopped pacing and came to stand directly in front of him. "Alex wasn't answering his phone. Something must've happened to him. I need to at least call my Supervisor to let her know I'm all right."

"You're not calling anyone, because you don't know who to trust. Right now, whoever these people are think we're dead, and we need to stay dead until we figure out why they came after you."

The color drained from her pretty brown face and he nodded his head, knowingly.

"You already know why."

She sat on the edge of the bed directly in front of him. "I guessed it as we drove away from the house. I just didn't want to believe it."

She exhaled a long sigh. "The Senator's wife is in protective custody because she's in possession of a payoff list—a list she kept for her husband that has the names of judges, attorneys, and cops who took bribes to look the other way in his illegal activity. She began to assemble it when she started handling his finances. But to ensure her safety, it was made public that she mailed the only copy to the District Attorney's office in Seattle. It was sealed in evidence, but a week later, it was stolen and destroyed."

"So, the case went bust?" he asked.

"Not quite. I know Mrs. McIntyre. We became friends in college shortly after you and I…broke up."

Roman shifted in his seat, not wanting to broach that topic right now.

"We both majored in Finance, had a lot of classes together and kept in touch after graduation. She knew I worked for the agency and without telling anyone, she sent me a copy of the payoff list."

Roman flinched. "You have a copy? The only remaining copy?"

"Yes."

"Who else knows you have it?"

"Just Alex and the Supervising agent in IAB."

"Then it's likely one of them is trying to kill you."

"That's the first thing I thought, but neither of their names are on the list."

Roman shrugged. "Then they could be protecting someone. Or maybe one of them was offered a big enough bribe to take you out."

She narrowed her eyes. "You mean like you?"

He walked right into that. "Fine. Let's talk about me. Where do I fit in? What was the point of this whole operation if you already had Mrs. McIntyre in protective custody?"

That was Alex's idea. Your ex-partner, Harry Rogers was on the list. Alex had been investigating him for being on the take for over a year. When he had enough evidence for an arrest, Alex brought him in and offered him a deal if he named you, too."

"Until last Tuesday, I never took a bribe in my career."

"I didn't think so, either. Your name wasn't on the list and there have never been any complaints or even whispers about you. But Alex—Agent Bailey—wasn't convinced. He was sure you two had a partnership taking bribes. He pursued the investigation on his own and asked me to join in to play the role of Mrs. McIntyre."

Admittedly, Roman was glad to know she wasn't the real

Mrs. McIntyre. It never sat well that she married a corrupt politician and got creative with his finances. It didn't strike him as the kind of woman she was. But then again, he never thought he would ever be the type of man to take a bribe. People changed, especially after fifteen years. Since setting eyes on her again, he caught himself wondering what she'd done since leaving college. In particular, he was interested to learn if she'd ever fallen in love since him. But the selfish side of him didn't like the idea of her with any other man, giving him her heart. He'd been lucky enough to have her heart, only he gave it back.

"You knew who I was long before this operation," he said.

"I didn't know until Alex told me who Harry Rogers' partner was. I recognized the name, looked you up in the directory and your photo and profile came up."

"And still you agreed to set me up."

"It's my job," she said, sounding defensive. "Agent Bailey and I worked together on a lot of cases. He had a hunch about you, and his hunches are rarely wrong."

"You had no evidence that I ever took a bribe, but you still went through with it. My lawyer will have a field day with this."

"You didn't have to take the money. If you had walked away, it would've ended there," she said, her voice rising.

"Would it? Or would *Alex* just bide his time, waiting to dangle another carrot in my face?"

She threw up her hands and stood from the bed. "We can argue about this all day, but the best thing to do is rest up and then head back to San Francisco. I need to be debriefed and hand over this list."

He chuckled scornfully. "You really don't get it, do you? You're just determined to walk out of here and get yourself killed. Well, you know what, go ahead. It's Christmas Eve, and I have a plane to catch." He stood, went to the bed and zipped up his duffel. He then yanked at the straps and headed for the door. "You can take the SUV with you back to San Francisco. I'll call a cab from the front office to take me to the airport."

She gaped at him. "Are you crazy? You're not going anywhere. You're under arrest!"

"You have bigger things to worry about. Did you ever ask yourself why you were the one ordered to be my decoy and why my instructions were to take you to that house? It was all a setup from the beginning."

That gave her pause.

"You made a phone call and told them we were there. The people you trust may not be on that list, but it's damaging enough to them to want to take you out."

She pulled her gun from her holster and aimed it at him. "All of that may be true, but I can't let you go, Roman."

"Yes, you can, because your case against me is going to get thrown out and besides, the other half of the money was burned up in the house."

When she still didn't lower her gun, his patience ran out and he exploded.

"As soon as I tell them about us, that will be it! Do you really want me to do that? Do you want me to tell them that I used to fuck my arresting agent back in college, and that she's still hurt from me dumping her for another woman?"

A bright sheen of tears came to the corners of her eyes, but he knew she'd never let them fall in front of him.

"Fuck you!" She gritted. "Get out of here."

Roman stood there, shocked into immobility. He couldn't believe the vicious words he'd just spoken, and there was no way to take them back.

He stepped toward her, the apology already on the tip of his tongue. "Dana, I'm—"

"Get. Out."

The gun was still steady and trained on him, and he had no doubt that if he made another step, tried to console her or explain himself, she would shoot him. He slowly returned to the door, opened it and looked back at her one last time. He had to say something, but from the look of rage and raw pain in her eyes, he'd already said more than enough.

CHAPTER FOURTEEN

California State University, April 2002

Dana walked out of the business school building to find Roman standing there waiting for her just like he always did. It was spring for the rest of the country, but in northern California the chill wasn't letting up. It was a shame, because she had some spring dresses she wanted to wear to show off her legs for Roman. Instead, she continued to opt for jeans and lightweight sweaters while fantasizing about this summer when it would be just a bit warmer. Thinking of summer had her wondering about the plans they would make before their senior year began. She wanted to go home and look for a job, and he'd said he was doing the same. Maybe they can see each other on their off days, and just the thought of them spending more time together had her feeling stupidly giddy inside.

She was smiling when she walked up to him, but it slowly faded away when she got close enough to see sadness and a bit of apprehension in his eyes.

"What's wrong?"

He took the books she was holding from her and gestured for her to follow him. "Let's talk."

Instantly, she was on guard. Roman didn't talk. He said what he needed to say, and listened indulgently while she rambled on about anything and everything. Most times, he was kissing her neck while she talked and then turned her mouth to his when he wanted her quiet. Also, she'd never seen this look on his face. He was carefree and easygoing. Not since his breakup with Kyra did anything much faze him. But something was wrong.

She trailed beside him through the busy campus until they came to a community garden given to the students and faculty. It was a quiet and secluded spot that spanned about a half an acre and doubled as a walking path with park benches. By the time Roman told her to sit down, Dana was convinced she didn't want to hear this.

He sat down beside her and looked out at the garden. "Kyra called me."

Dana breathed in and out and told herself to stay calm. There was still a chance this could all be innocent. "What did she want?"

"She asked how I was doing and wanted to see how my classes were going." He paused. "She wanted to meet me for an early breakfast, and I agreed. That's why I didn't see you last night. I had to get up early and I didn't want to disturb you."

"You didn't want to explain where you were going," she amended.

He looked at her and shame covered his face and filled those dusky gray eyes. "Yeah."

"So, what did she want, or do I even have to ask?"

"She broke up with that guy—"

"The one she dumped you for?"

"Dana."

They both went silent for a while, watching a student water the tulips that were just beginning to bloom.

"You're going to think I'm a real asshole, and I am, but the truth is I was never fully over her. She asked me to give her another chance and—"

"Don't," she said, raising a hand. "Please, don't say another word."

"You mean so much to me."

"Stop, Roman."

"Dana, I told her I would."

She turned to him, took his face between her hands and kissed him softly. It was her turn to shut him up.

Just kiss me. Kiss me until everything you just said disappears.

She felt one arm go around her waist, and he returned the kiss with a fervor she'd never felt from him before. He tasted every inch of her mouth as if savoring its feel and fullness, and she knew what he was doing. He was memorizing her, because this was a goodbye kiss.

His arms fell from her waist, and his hands grasped her wrists.

"I'm sorry," he said, and then slowly pulled away from her, rose from the bench and left.

ana sat on the bed, reading the email Alex sent, and then thought about her next move. After Roman left, she pulled out her laptop, connected it to the motor lodge's WIFI and sent Alex an email, telling him what happened that morning. He said he would be taking a flight into Seattle that evening and agreed to meet with her an hour away from the motor lodge. She could only give him the condensed version of what happened, but nevertheless, he promised to keep this between the two of them and assured her he'd get her to safety until they figured out what was going on and how deep the corruption went.

When he asked about Agent Walsh, she typed back it was a long story and would fill him in when she saw him. Truthfully, she was just buying time, because she had no idea how she was going to explain to him that she allowed an agent in her custody to just walk away.

She checked the time on her computer and saw it was now late afternoon. Roman should be back in California by now to see his kids and although she respected his dedication as a father, she wasn't so sure she wouldn't shoot him if she ever saw him again. She'd risked her job in letting him go, but she risked her reputation even more if she pursued the arrest. The last thing she needed in a field dominated by men was any one of them thinking she was a scorned woman who shared kisses and more with the men in her custody. Just thinking about the backlash made her cringe with embarrassment.

Then the embarrassment was replaced with a hot rush of anger as she thought about Roman's parting words to her, but she couldn't decide what angered her more. Was it the fact he said it, or was it the fact that it might be true? Was she still carrying the pain of their breakup with her to the point it was affecting her judgment? She was so busy trying to secure his arrest that she hadn't even realized she was being set up by someone in her own department.

Her gut told her it had to be Alex, but she didn't have the least idea how she would go about getting him to admit it without getting herself killed in the process. She'd suspected him from the moment he didn't answer his phone just before the attack this morning, only she kept it to herself. However, Roman arrived at the same conclusion, which only confirmed her suspicions. Jesus, did all of that really happen only this morning—watching the parade, arresting Roman, the explosion? Now she was about to face a man she'd always considered to be a trustworthy colleague, when in reality, he'd been nothing more than her enemy. This had been one of the longest days of her life, and she vowed next year she would just sleep through Christmas.

* * *

Alex pulled up in his rental at the designated meeting spot about ten minutes after she did. When he saw her, he rushed out of his car and motioned for her to come to him. Dana felt the weight of her gun tucked securely in her holster, and climbed out of the SUV, keeping her coat wrapped tight around her to shield from the biting wind.

"Are you all right?" he asked when she approached him.

She nodded. "Just confused. I know this all has to do with the list, but I can't figure out who would want to kill me for it."

"Listen," Alex said, beginning to pace back and forth in an effort to stay warm. "I think it would be safer if you hand the list over to me. I told you to do this before, but you didn't listen to me. Now look what's happened. Our investigation was compromised, and you were nearly killed. As long as that list is in your possession, you're in danger. I'll see that it gets to the DA."

She shook her head. "I can't do that. Whoever is trying to kill me believes I have this list. Whether I give it to you or not, I'm in danger. I'd rather be in danger and have leverage."

He persisted. "I told you I'll make sure you're safe."

"What happened to Adams and Russo? They were supposed to be my backup but never showed."

Impatience crept across his face. "The GPS got them turned around. They said by the time they got to you, the house was in flames and you and Walsh were nowhere to be found." He narrowed his gaze at the SUV behind her. "Speaking of Walsh, isn't that his car?"

"Yes."

"Where is he?"

She tucked her hands into her pockets and raised her chin slightly. "I let him go."

He stared at her dumbfounded. "You let him go? Why the hell would you do that?"

She didn't answer him, but instead continued with her

own questioning. "You want the list so bad, Alex? Then level with me. What is it about Agent Walsh? You have this special interest in him that I can't understand. His partner, Harry was guilty. His name is on the Senator's bribe list. But Roman? Help me understand. You've been keeping me out of the loop from the beginning and then only using me for your agenda." She paused to look around the deserted road. "It's just us out here. Tell me what the hell is going on."

He regarded her for a moment, and she assumed he was weighing in his mind the pros and cons of confiding in her. Finally, he expelled a long breath.

"Harry and I were working together. We were both on the Senator's payroll, but only Harry was listed. He was arrested because he was sloppy and getting reckless. But when I brought him in, he told me others knew about our arrangement with the Senator. I assumed he was talking about his partner. I couldn't risk my involvement getting out, so I had to find a way to get rid of Walsh, too. That's when I set up this sting operation."

Dana had assumed he was involved somehow, but actually hearing the words stunned her.

"And you tried to kill me in the process," she said.

He snatched his gun out and aimed it at her. It was such a quick move that it would've surprised her if she hadn't been expecting it. He was a desperate man, and killing her and leaving her on the side of the road in this wintry night would be nothing to him. She was a loose string he couldn't afford to keep dangling.

"You wouldn't give up the list," he said. "I thought when I paid to have it stolen from the DA's office and destroyed, that was the end of it. Imagine my shock when you come to me saying you have a copy. That list is my link to Harry, and by extension, to Senator McIntyre. Without it, Harry can scream to the heavens that I was his partner, but no one is going to believe a dirty fed."

"I trusted you," she said.

The gun remained steady in his hands. "I know you did, and I'm sorry about all of this. You're a good agent, Dana. You just got in the way. I don't want to shoot you, but I will unless you hand over that list now."

"I hand it over, and I'm dead anyway."

He was silent, and she knew she guessed the truth.

"Just give it to me," he said, holding a gloved hand out. "Give it to me!"

She raised one hand and slowly reached into her coat pocket. "It's right here. I'm reaching for it."

But she was actually reaching for her gun, estimating in her head how much time she had to get one shot off, before he could. She felt the hard metal against her gloved hand and all she had to do was grip the handle. Would it be enough time?

But something caught her attention. There was a shadowed figure coming up behind Alex, and she couldn't resist glancing slightly over his shoulder. Alex noticed her distraction, and his instincts had him whirling around to fire. But the figure stalking him already had a gun raised and fired first. Alex stumbled back, but still tried to get at his attacker. Dana ducked down, grabbed her gun from her holster and shot Alex several times in the back. His torso jerked back and forth as he received gunfire from both sides. Then both Dana and the other shooter stopped firing and Alex fell to his knees and then face first onto the deserted road.

Dana kept her gun trained on his lifeless, bloody body and then raised the gun to the shadowed figure who was now walking under the street lamp, revealing his face as he jammed another clip into his gun.

"Are you all right?" Roman asked.

She nodded, slowly lowering her weapon and not sure how she felt about seeing him. "Yeah."

"Good," he said, reaching out his hand to help her up. "Let's get out of here."

CHAPTER SIXTEEN

She'd gone quiet, but Roman didn't think it was from shock. More than likely, she was just exhausted. It was the second time in less than 24 hours that someone tried to kill her, and she was likely feeling the mental and physical effects from it all. Every now and then, he'd look over at her, but she kept still and quiet and simply stared out the window at the darkened sky and trees whizzing by.

After another twenty minutes of silence, he finally heard her speak softly.

"I thought you went back to California."

He looked her way briefly and then focused once again on the two-lane highway that would take them back to the motor lodge.

"That's what I needed you to think. I was sure it was someone in your office out to get you, and I knew you wouldn't be able to resist making contact."

"So where did you go?"

"I have a spare key to the SUV. I stayed crouched in the

backseat under a blanket and waited until either you left or someone came to see you."

She seemed to ponder that and then spoke again.

"Alex told me everything. He must have figured I would be dead soon anyway and didn't see any risk in confessing." She paused and sighed heavily. "I can't trust anyone."

When they arrived back at the motor lodge, Roman did a lap to check out any cars that seemed out of place. He also went into the room first to inspect it before finally letting Dana come inside. When she stepped into the room, she still looked to be in a daze. She went to the bed, sat down on the edge with her coat still on and watched as he secured the room. He locked and bolted the door, checked to make sure the windows were locked, and then withdrew his gun and clip and put them beside the bed.

He left her briefly to use the bathroom, and when he came out, she was still in the same place, looking completely lost. He went over to her and stood directly in front of her.

"Dana."

She'd been staring at a space on the opposite wall and at the sound of her name, she slowly raised her brown eyes to meet his.

"You can trust me."

She didn't say anything, but returned her attention to the spot on the wall. He took hold of her shoulders, stood her up from the bed and helped her out of her coat and undid her gun holster. She didn't move the entire time, perfectly content with allowing him to take control.

With her coat and gun holster in hand, he tried to move to the side to lay them on a desk chair beside the bed, but Dana stepped in front of him. He moved to the other side and she matched his steps, blocking his path.

That's when he looked down at her and she was staring

up at him, her face so close that all he had to do was move an inch and her lips would be all his. She must've been thinking the same thing, because she was now fixated on his mouth.

"Why does this always happen?" she asked, mostly to herself. "Why am I always drawn to you? Why can't I stay away?"

She moved her eyes up to meet his.

"Don't deny me this again," she said.

She stood on her tip toes and hesitantly touched his lips softly to hers, and then stopped and looked at him. When he didn't object, she did it again, keeping her eyes open watching him watching her kiss him. The third time, Roman had had enough. He tossed her coat and holster somewhere in the vicinity of the chair and wrapped his arms around her waist to bring her up against him. He devoured her, delving his tongue in deep, which made them both moan from anticipation.

Dana immediately started to wrestle with his t-shirt and broke the kiss long enough to bring it over his head. She then took off her own shirt while he shed his jeans. By the time she was down to just her bra and panties, he lifted her soft and pliant body and practically tossed her on the bed. He crawled on top of her, slipped down her bra straps and released her beautiful breasts. He cupped them both in his hands and licked and sucked painstakingly slow. He looked up to find her watching him, her eyes glazed over with pleasure as the excitement built within her. She then wriggled free of her panties and as he moved from her breasts to her neck and shoulders, he shoved off his own underwear. When he couldn't wait any longer, he sat up, spread her legs apart with his knees and got comfortable in between her thighs. He was rock hard for her—hell, he had been for days when he first set eyes on her in the townhouse.

He never thought he'd see her again, and somewhere in the back of his mind, buried deep, that fact saddened him. He hated the way he'd left things with them—the way he just got up from that park bench, leaving her friendship and her love for him behind.

And he'd done it again this afternoon, only this time, he left in his wake angry and ugly words, making her believe he was a man who would just abandon her at every turn. He was determined to rid that image of him in her mind. Starting here at this moment, he'd make her feel safe. He'd show her just how much he wanted her and missed her.

"Where are you?" she asked.

He watched as she moved seductively beneath him with her legs spread and waiting for him. The sight nearly undid him.

"I'm right here. I'm not going anywhere."

With that, he plunged himself into that part of her that was so hot, wet and inviting.

"Roman," she cried out in delight as he stroked in and out of her.

She closed her eyes and grabbed for the headboard, leaving her breasts exposed and daring him to have his way with her. He leaned down and flicked each nipple with his tongue while he continued to rock in and out of her. Fifteen years had gone by, since he'd been with her intimately, and he couldn't get over how good she felt to him. She felt even better, and as he moved inside of her, he became dangerously close to losing himself, just like he did in his 20's. He couldn't get enough of her, and it scared him. It was in part why he went back to Kyra. She was safe and predictable, whereas with Dana, he felt as if he were under a spell, a force he couldn't break free from.

"Don't stop, Roman. Give it to me," she cried. "Give it all to me!"

And he did. Several more strokes, and they both could no longer take the overwhelming pleasure. They came together and as he roared out her name, it was akin to a declaration. He didn't care what she did to him—just as long as it always felt like this.

CHAPTER SEVENTEEN

"What do we do now, Roman?"

They were spooned together in bed, and he had his arms wrapped around her breasts while kissing her neck and shoulders, waiting for that moment when sleep would overpower her. He wanted her to fall asleep in his arms, knowing he was still there.

"We get some sleep, and then pack up and leave in the morning."

She turned her head slightly to look over her shoulder at him. "And go where?"

"The DA's home just outside of Seattle. We need to deliver that payoff list personally. I'm also going to make damn sure she puts you in protective custody until every one of those names are released. You won't be safe until it all goes public."

"They'll probably put me in the same place with Sarah."

"Sarah?"

"Sarah McIntyre. That's the Senator's wife."

He frowned. "There was nothing in the report about her name being Sarah. It was always Dana. Unless…"

She turned her body fully around to face him, and when he saw the look of regret flash in her eyes, he already knew the answer.

"We fed you information, Roman. All the reports you received came directly from IAB. It was just luck on our part that you never did any outside research."

He let out a self-deprecating laugh. "Why would I? My mind was just on that payout."

She reached out her hand to stroke his cheek, but he jerked away from her touch.

"Don't. Don't do that. I don't want or deserve your compassion. I took a bribe at the expense of a witness. I sacrificed everything I stood for as an agent for a measly bit of cash."

"I didn't want to do this in the first place," she said. "I never wanted to investigate you. When I realized who you were, all of those memories from college came back, and I just wanted to forget them and move on."

He sighed, took her by the waist and pulled her on top of him.

"I've made a fucking mess of things." He kissed her and then made sure she had his attention. "I want you to promise me something. When we get into Seattle tomorrow and all the questioning starts, you make sure you tell them every-thing. Understand? Everything. Don't try to protect me or what I did."

She snorted with derision. "What do you want me to do? Arrest you as soon as I get out of protective custody? We've slept together. The case is over."

"They'll never hear that from me," he insisted. The two of us here together, the fact that we dated in college—none of it will ever come out."

She shook her head. "I can't. I won't. Think of your kids.

You could go to jail. You'll lose your career. It was Alex's case anyway, and he's dead. Let's forget about it."

"It's what I deserve," he said, squeezing her tight. "Whether he's dead or not, whether he was just looking to set me up, none of it matters. I took that bribe, and none of this is your fault. You were doing your job. You were being a good agent."

"Roman, please."

He kissed her again, not wanting her to say anymore. He kissed her long and deep, running his fingers through her hair, committing her sweet taste to his memory. It would be the second time he kissed her goodbye.

CHAPTER EIGHTEEN

Saturday, December 25th

The next morning, they checked out of the motor lodge early and drove to the outskirts of Seattle where the District Attorney, Tina Lowell resided. After apologizing for disturbing her Christmas with her family, Dana handed her the only remaining copy of Senator McIntyre's bribery list in exchange for temporary protective custody.

"Come with me," DA Lowell said and ushered them both into her home office where she began making calls to her contacts in the FBI who she trusted and disrupted their Christmas as well. Then the clock started ticking. An investigation was immediately opened within the FBI's California Internal Affairs division to determine who else besides Agent Alex Bailey was in on the attempt on Dana's life.

Both Dana and Roman were held separately in questioning for hours to detail the events of the cabin and the shooting death of Agent Bailey.

They questioned Dana first, and Roman sat impatiently in his interview room waiting for his turn to reveal the truth about his involvement. Two hours later, an agent came in.

"Agent Walsh, we got your statement and it corroborates with Agent Corbin's regarding Agent Bailey and his attempted murder."

Roman nodded.

"You also claim that the house you and Agent Corbin went to was a trap, and she corroborates that as well. We have an APB out on those men. More than likely, they were hired by Agent Bailey. We're going through his home and office now to see if we can find a connection to them."

The agent looked through his notes some more and then nodded his head with finality. "All right. I think that's all for now. You can go home. We have your contact information if we need anything further from you."

"Wait a minute, you don't have it all," Roman said. "Did she tell you why I was with her in the first place?"

He flipped through the folder and came to a document that must have been Dana's official statement.

"Agent Corbin states you were escorting her to Seattle to give the DA the payoff list and that her department instructed the two of you to go to the house and wait for more backup. Gunfire was exchanged, the house exploded and you saved her life, twice."

"No, listen. I took a bribe. I took a bribe and was told to take her to that house. This was all supposed to be apart of a sting operation set up by Agent Bailey. Dana—I mean—Agent Corbin would have arrested me if we hadn't been attacked."

The man stared at him with a raised brow. He then cleared his throat and leaned forward. "Look, I don't know what you're talking about, and to be honest, I don't want to know. We've already received a full statement from Agent Corbin. She says you were escorting her and you saved her life. End of story. As far as I'm concerned and as far as she's concerned, whatever you did or didn't do, is forgotten.

Whatever Agent Bailey was doing died with him. Let it go, consider yourself forgiven and enjoy what's left of your Christmas. I'm sure you have a family waiting on you."

"I want to see her," Roman demanded.

The agent shook his head, gathered up the folders and stood. "I can't do that. She's already in protective custody. No one is getting to her until that list goes out. We want to keep her safe. Merry Christmas, Agent Walsh."

CHAPTER NINETEEN

"*D*addy!"

Roman set the presents down by the door just before Brianna and Tyler plowed into him with the biggest hugs their small arms could give him. He hugged and kissed them both back, gathered them in his arms and lifted them into the air to continue into the large ranch-style home. On his way into the large open family room, he was met with an assortment of Kyra's family: brothers, sisters, cousins, aunts and uncles, nephews and nieces and of course her parents. They all greeted him with warm smiles and Christmas cheer. He returned each greeting, and as he looked at the beaming smiles on his son and daughter's faces, he realized he had made the right choice in putting aside his pride and making the trip to see them. A lump lodged somewhere in his throat when he thought how his foolish actions could have taken him away from them forever. Dana had prevented that, and he wanted so desperately to tell her in person how he would be forever grateful to her.

As he sat his kids down in front of the oversized and beautifully decorated Christmas tree with the other children, he realized he'd left their presents at the front door. He turned and saw Kyra standing behind him, smiling and holding the bag of gifts.

"Thank you," he said, taking them from her and calling Brianna and Tyler over to open their presents.

"Come see what Santa brought you," he said, bending down to kiss them both on their round cheeks.

As he watched them tear into the gift-wrapping, Kyra came to sit down on the couch beside him.

"I'm glad you could make it," she said. "They really missed you."

"Yeah. When I get a chance, I'll thank your parents later for having me."

"So, I take it everything went well with the witness," she said. "Did you get them safely to protective custody?"

Dana.

He hated the thought of her in some safe house on Christmas Day. He wanted her here with him. He wanted to be with her. Maybe they could do something for new year's together with his kids.

With a start, he realized he was making plans to be with her, but a warm feeling embraced him when he continued to think about the future with her in it.

"Yeah, everything worked out fine. She's safe."

"*She?*" Kyra reiterated.

Roman took his attention off his kids for just a moment and looked at her. "Yeah. She. Is there a problem?"

She laughed at herself. "I'm sorry. Old habits. I've always been jealous of every new woman in your life, especially when we're not together."

"Are you serious?"

She nodded. "I know it's stupid and makes me look like a hypocrite, but when I get wind that you might be involved with someone else or if even if you're just working with another woman, I just think about how lucky they are. You're a loyal and giving man. I guess I just could never appreciate it when I had you."

He chuckled. "We were together for years, Kyra. There haven't been many women in my life besides you."

"There were a few," she countered. "But one in particular had me really worried. We went to high school with her and then college. She was African-American and I think she and I had the same math class. Diane, Dina, or something like that."

"Dana," he said without thinking.

She snapped her fingers. "That's right. You had a thing going with her for a few months, but the way you looked whenever I saw you two together had me thinking I'd lost you for good."

"But you hadn't lost me," he said. "Like a puppy dog, I came right back as soon as you called."

"Don't be like that, Roman," she said, hearing the resentment in his voice. "We were kids. A bunch of immature kids, and I was selfish for trying to take you back when you were clearly happy with her."

She paused and looked at their children playing with their new gifts. "I don't regret our marriage, because the best thing that came out of it were Bri and Tyler. But there are a lot of days I sit and wonder what would've happened if I'd just left you alone."

Over the years, since college, he'd wondered about that, too, but not for long. If things had gone differently, he wouldn't have his children. Besides, there was no point in trying to rewrite the past. He'd been given a second chance, when he could've lost everything. Now, he just wanted to move forward.

"Anyway, I'm glad you're here, because there's something I wanted to give you," she said.

She pulled a packet of papers from behind her back and handed them to him.

"I was talking to my parents, and they convinced me I was being unreasonable and, once again, selfish. This is an amended custody agreement. It gives you weekends and summers and we'll alternate holidays. I know your job can keep you busy, so if there's a weekend you have to work, just let me know."

He clutched the papers in his hands and then looked up at her feeling gratitude wash over him.

"Thank you, Kyra."

She shrugged, giving him a warm smile. "You're a great dad, and they deserve to be with you as much as possible. Merry Christmas."

"Merry Christmas," he said, smiling and then sat down on the floor to play with his children and their new toys.

CHAPTER TWENTY

riday, January 7th

Dana came home at precisely 7:22 that evening. She entered her apartment, turned and closed the door and leaned her head back against it, shutting her eyes and in effect, shutting out the rest of the world. She moved away from the door, kicked off her heels and untucked her blouse from her skirt. She practically threw her purse and coat onto an armchair and then finally tumbled onto the sofa where she planned to stay for the rest of the weekend. She was so exhausted, it nearly brought her to tears.

On Monday, December 27th, Senator Robert McIntyre's payoff list was given to a grand jury and by the end of that day, every news media outlet had published the story and a few of the names had been leaked. Since then, Dana's life had been in a tailspin with debriefings back to back with not just the FBI, but also the DA's office. She was required to schedule and attend several sessions with the department Psychiatrist since she was involved in Agent Alex Bailey's shooting. Things had let up a bit during the New Years' weekend, but then were back in full effect on January 3rd, especially since the Grand Jury had issued multiple indictments against the Senator and those on his bribery list. Those who had been arrested were making deals left and right, turning on each other and the Senator for a reduced sentence. Dana's name had been, for the most part, kept out of the media and she had the DA's office and the FBI to thank for that. After all, it had all begun with Sarah McIntyre bringing the infamous list to light in the first place. Dana just happened to have a copy.

Still, just because the media wasn't hounding her door didn't mean she was exempt from questioning altogether. She'd just come from her latest interview with the head of Internal Affairs, where she'd once again gone over everything that took place from the moment Agent Roman Walsh picked her up to escort her to Washington.

Her official statement remained the same which was that she'd made the mistake of trusting Agent Bailey and confiding in him about the list. He plotted her death by instructing Agent Walsh to take her to a safe house that was not official. Agent Walsh saved her from both the explosion and from Agent Bailey himself when he tried to kill her again.

That was all she would ever say. She'd been sure to send a text to Roman telling him that would be her official statement, and she hoped he stuck to it as well.

She looked over at the Christmas tree in the corner of the living room, still decorated with a mix of red, green, gold and silver ornaments and tinsel. She got up to turn the lights on and then lay back down to admire it. She never put presents underneath, because she didn't have many people in her life to give gifts. She'd visit her mother, they would have a nice dinner and then watch a movie together. Afterwards, Dana would go home, turn on her Christmas tree lights and then sit in front of it, just as she was doing now, and enjoying the peace it gave her.

Her doorbell rang, instantly disturbing that peace. God, she hoped it wasn't one of her superiors wanting to make a house call for an impromptu interview. She rose from the couch and trudged to the door, not caring about her disheveled appearance. She peered through the peephole, saw who it was and stepped back, stunned.

"Let me in," she heard him say on the other side.

She opened the door, took one long look at him filling her doorway and stepped to the side. Roman walked in and looked around.

"I figured the fancy address in Pacific Heights was a cover. What about the security guard?"

She closed the door and came up to stand behind him, watching as he observed her much smaller and simpler home.

"That house belongs to Sarah. Curtis is really her security. She gave us permission to use both the home and Curtis in the investigation."

He turned around to face her, and she had to back up slightly. "You went to a lot of trouble with that investigation. It's a shame to let it go like you did."

"I told you, it was never my investigation to begin with. It was all a set up on Alex's part to put you in jail and kill me." She stepped around him and went back to sit on the couch. "Why are you here Roman, and how did you even know where I lived?"

He put his hands in the pockets of his jeans. "I saw you leave work and followed you.

"You followed me? Why?"

"Why do you think? I haven't seen you since Christmas. They separated us for every questioning and debriefing…I was worried."

"Didn't you get my text? I told you what I was going to say. No need to worry, because your career remains intact."

A cloud of anger shadowed his eyes. "I was worried about you. And I never asked for your protection. If you recall, I told you to tell them the truth. I never would've…" He paused, looked around and then back at her. "Look, I know you're tired. You had a shitty Christmas and New Year, but it'll all be over soon."

"And then what?" She asked, looking up at him.

"What do you mean?"

"I mean what happens with us? Are you going to call me, go on a few dates with me, and invite me into your bed?"

"All those possibilities have crossed my mind."

"And then what?"

He shrugged. "I don't know. Does it matter?"

She rose from the couch and headed for the door. "Good-bye, Roman."

He whirled around and took hold of her arm just as she passed by him. "Stop. What just happened?"

She jerked her arm free. "I'm not going to do this again. I'm not going to be with you, fall in love with you, plan a life with you and risk you ripping it all away from me again!"

"Dana—"

"You were right, you know? You said I'm still hurt from you dumping me in college. Well it's true, and I don't care how ridiculous it sounds. It fucking hurts, because I loved you!"

She looked away from his surprised expression and chuckled derisively. "You know what's even more ridiculous? I never stopped loving you. It's probably why I agreed to play Sarah's decoy. I knew I'd be with you that holiday weekend, and I couldn't pass up the chance to see you again and be near you. Even if it was just to set you up."

"I'm glad it was you," he said quietly.

She scoffed. "Stop it, Roman."

"I mean it," he said. "I'm glad you were with me. That week is the first time in a long time I didn't feel like my life was crap. I had this job and kids I only saw part-time. There was nothing else. Okay, so you're motives for being with me were all a lie, but you were still with me, and I wouldn't trade a minute of it."

"Please just go," she said. "You're only saying all of this now, because you feel like you owe me for not arresting you. Well you don't have to feel obligated to me in any way. You saved my life. Consider us even."

"You're wrong."

"I want you to leave."

"Why?" he erupted. "Why do you keep pushing me away?"

"No, the question is why do I keep falling for you, when you'll never choose me?"

He grabbed hold of her shoulders. "But I am choosing you."

"For how long?"

"For as long as you'll have me. Please, Dana. It was a mistake to leave you all those years ago. You were the right woman for me, but I was a dumb kid who thought he knew what he wanted, and I didn't know shit. You weren't just my girlfriend. You were my friend. All those years with Kyra, I felt something was missing, and it was friendship. No, screw that, it wasn't just friendship, it was you."

He released her and stepped away. "It was missing you."

Tears that she thought she'd shed a long time ago came back in a flood, and he pulled her into his arms, holding her tight. She felt him resting his chin on the top of her head, and that simple gesture gave her more peace than she could ever get from looking at her Christmas tree.

"Please don't give up, now," he spoke softly into her hair.

"Not now when I finally realized I love you. I've always loved you."

She pulled back to look at him and gave him a weak smile. She knew her face looked a mess smudged with tears, but she didn't care.

"So, what do we do now?"

He laughed. "What is it with you and that question?"

She shrugged one shoulder. "I like to stay one step ahead."

He kissed her forehead and looked over at the Christmas tree. "Do you have anything to drink in the house?"

"Egg nog."

"That'll do. Go get it and some blankets and pillows."

She returned with the items along with a carton of egg nog and two wine glasses. She handed him the pillow and blankets and watched as he laid them out under the Christmas tree. He then promptly began to remove his shirt and shed his jeans.

"What are you doing?" she asked, both surprised and excited.

"You never really had your Christmas. Go turn on some music, take your clothes off and come lay beside me."

"What?"

He stepped over to her, shoved her skirt up and palmed her ass. "Fine. Leave your clothes on," he said. "I have plenty of ways to get to you."

In a matter of minutes, he was lying on his back, gripping Dana's waist as she rode him. He let her take all of the stress from the past two weeks out on his body. She rocked her hips back and forth, reaching for that sublime moment when she was finally able to release everything in a torrent of ecstasy, and calling out his name as it all swept away.

An hour later, Christmas carols were playing softly through her iPod speakers as the two of them lay together wrapped in warm blankets under the tree with half empty glasses of egg nog beside them and their clothes in a tangled heap.

"If I knew we'd end up like this under the tree, I would've at least bought you a present," she said, snuggling close to him.

"There's plenty of time for that," he said, his arm wrapped around her shoulder and lightly caressing her arm.

"Is there?" she asked, still feeling slight trepidation.

He put his forefinger to her chin and tilted her head up to look at him. "I meant what I said on Christmas Eve. I'm here, and I'm not going anywhere."

A smile creased her lips, because something deep inside urged her to believe him. "Well then…Merry Christmas, Roman."

He lowered his head, kissed her lips and indulged himself until she moaned with wanting. Before they got too carried away, he slowly pulled back and brushed her hair from her face. His gray eyes held so much warmth as he looked at her.

"Merry Christmas and happy new year, Dana. Next year, I promise to say it on time. And the year after that. And the year after that."

* * *

Thank you for reading EX O EX O! If you enjoyed Roman and Dana's exciting love story, you'll love the next book in the EX FILES series, EXPOSED.

When married couple Eric and Havilland Sawyer find themselves on opposite sides of a high-profile investigation, what could possibly go wrong?

Everything.

ONE-CLICK EXPOSED NOW >

"A plot twist you do not see coming."

"This book will take you on a ride and just when you think you've figured everything out, she surprises you and takes you in a different direction."

SIGN UP FOR LISA'S NEWSLETTER:

www.lisaryancampbell.com/newsletter

And if you love a springtime romance with suspense, make sure you check out EX APPEAL, an EX FILES novella.

Ava never thought she'd return to Gypsy Bay, but she did and her job is to investigate the unsolved murder of Michelle Meyer. But all the evidence is pointing to one person and the reason Ava left town in the first place…Michelle's husband.

"Loved, loved, loved this book!"

"Loved the suspense, danger, twists and turns!"

"I haven't been this intrigued by a book for awhile…this was phenomenal!"

ONE-CLICK EX APPEAL for a steamy and suspenseful read.

ABOUT THE AUTHOR

Award-winning Author, Lisa Ryan Campbell began writing as a small child using her mother's pink typewriting paper. Years later, she decided it was important to get a "real job" and attended Arizona State University to major in English with the goal of continuing on for both a Master's and Doctorate degrees in English and teach at the college level.

In 2002, Lisa graduated with a Bachelor's degree in English Literature and an Ancient Egyptian romance novel she wrote in her spare time. She decided then she would not be continuing on to graduate school, but instead joined Romance Writers of America and focused on her true love.

Lisa is an avid traveler and has seen many of the world's treasures in Egypt, Peru, Spain, France, Morocco, England, Mexico and the Caribbean. She spends her time mostly at her home in Colorado writing, reading and watching 1940's noir movies. She also loves to laugh, so you may frequently catch her watching reruns of Archer, Veep and The Office.

Sign up for Lisa's newsletter and find out more about her books at www.Lisaryancampbell.com and connect with her on social media.